Dear Parents:

Congratulations! Your child is taking the first steps on an exciting journey. The destination? Independent reading!

STEP INTO READING® will help your child get there. The program offers five steps to reading success. Each step includes fun stories and colorful art or photographs. In addition to original fiction and books with favorite characters, there are Step into Reading Non-Fiction Readers, Phonics Readers and Boxed Sets, Sticker Readers, and Comic Readers—a complete literacy program with something to interest every child.

Learning to Read, Step by Step!

Ready to Read   Preschool–Kindergarten
• big type and easy words • rhyme and rhythm • picture clues
For children who know the alphabet and are eager to begin reading.

Reading with Help   Preschool–Grade 1
• basic vocabulary • short sentences • simple stories
For children who recognize familiar words and sound out new words with help.

Reading on Your Own   Grades 1–3
• engaging characters • easy-to-follow plots • popular topics
For children who are ready to read on their own.

Reading Paragraphs   Grades 2–3
• challenging vocabulary • short paragraphs • exciting stories
For newly independent readers who read simple sentences with confidence.

Ready for Chapters   Grades 2–4
• chapters • longer paragraphs • full-color art
For children who want to take the plunge into chapter books but still like colorful pictures.

STEP INTO READING® is designed to give every child a successful reading experience. The grade levels are only guides; children will progress through the steps at their own speed, developing confidence in their reading.

Remember, a lifetime love of reading starts with a single step!

Step into Reading, Random House, and the Random House colophon are registered trademarks of Penguin Random House LLC.

Visit us on the Web!
StepIntoReading.com
randomhousekids.com

Educators and librarians, for a variety of teaching tools, visit us at RHTeachersLibrarians.com

ISBN 978-0-399-55692-0 (trade) — ISBN 978-0-399-55693-7 (lib. bdg.)

Printed in the United States of America
10 9 8 7 6 5 4 3 2 1

nickelodeon

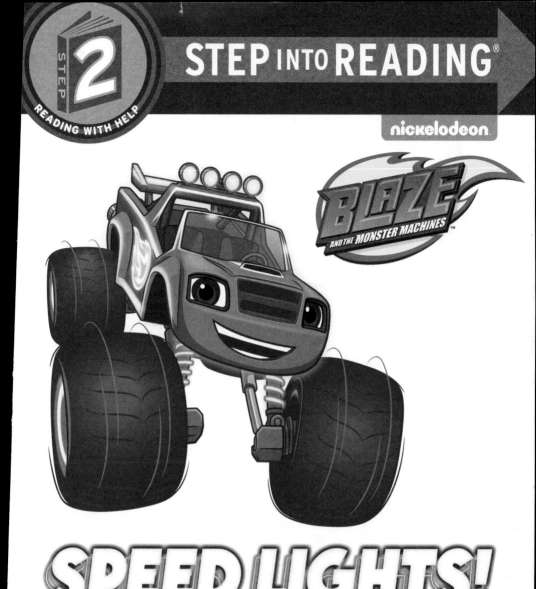

BLAZE AND THE MONSTER MACHINES™

SPEED LIGHTS!

by C. Ines Mangual

illustrated by Dynamo Limited

Random House 🏠 New York

Vroom!

Blaze and his friends

are ready to race at night!

The bright lights
help them
see the track.

The Light Thief

hops down the street.

She takes a streetlight!

The Light Thief
sees more lights
at the track.
They are big!

The Light Thief
steals the lights
from the track!

Oh, no!

The racers cannot see!

It is too dark.

They spin and crash.

Blaze gets
some speed lights.
They help him
see in the dark!

Blaze speeds off
to catch the Light Thief.

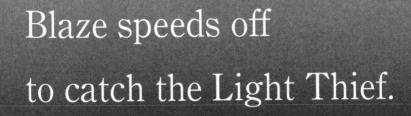

Blaze drives through

a dark tunnel.

Blaze follows
the Light Thief
to a scrap yard.

Metal pipes
fall down.
Blaze gets stuck!

Blaze turns himself
into a laser-blasting
Monster Machine!

Blaze uses his lasers
to cut the metal pipes.

Blaze chases

the Light Thief

to a bright carnival.

The Light Thief
steals all the
colorful lights!
Blaze needs help!

Blaze gets help
from his friends.
They have speed lights,
too!

The Light Thief
tries to hide.
Blaze spots her!

The Light Thief
wants all the lights
because she is afraid
of the dark!

AJ gives her
a light for her hat.
The Light Thief
is not afraid anymore!

The Light Thief
returns all the lights.
Blaze and his friends
can race again!